WESTERN DOG

By Carin Fox

Dedicated to my Mom, Beverly Fox,
who taught me everything is possible...

FOREWARD: NOTES FROM A PROUD SISTER:

My sister Carin and I grew up in the Bronx. Without a doubt, her favorite part of the Bronx was visiting our beloved local zoo. She had a love of animals from the very beginning, and throughout her writing, you can see and feel that connection.

Carin's writing is often from the point of view of her animal characters, so it allows the reader to be an insider to their emotions and thoughts.

Carin is a very descriptive writer as well. As I read her work, I am always able to picture the atmosphere that the characters are in. Their fears and their dreams. Many of her characters I feel I know as if they were close friends of mine.

Though her writing is filled with details, still, she always manages to keep me guessing as well. And as a sister, she always keeps me guessing too. I never quite know what she'll do next. And I always am anxious to find out.

I know her writing will transport you to another place, of fun adventures and new friends. I hope you enjoy the ride as I have.

With sincerest wishes & love,

Robin Fox (Carin's sister)

A Most Loyal Dog

A long time ago out in the west, there was a little yellow dog, who had straight hair, a long tail and down ears. This dog was well known in the nearby town as the most loyal dog ever. He was very helpful in the town. If you ever needed someone to listen to your problems, he was always there. If you needed something soft and cute to hold, he was happy to be with you. If you were sad or lonely, he was also happy to be with you. If you needed someone to cuddle with at night just so you wouldn't be scared, he was right there when you were ready to go to sleep. The people in the town thought that they were lucky to have such a loyal dog. The dog thought he was very lucky to be near a town that really appreciated what he did for them.

There were weird things about this dog too. He would always come into town wearing a cowboy hat, boots, and a bandana. He would also ride a zebra like a normal horse. Every morning he would wake up, go to the kitchen, open the cabinet, and get a can of dog food. Then after closing the cabinet, he would place the can in the can opener and with his front right paw, carefully open the can. He would then put the food in his food bowl and eat a hearty breakfast.

After breakfast he would go outside with a bridle and a saddle. Now, putting a bridle and a saddle on a zebra is not easy. Yellow Dog had to first climb onto a fence just to be able to reach the zebra. Soon enough he would be ready to go to town, but first he had to select which hat and bandana he was going to wear that day. His hats and bandanas were kept under the fifth board of his front porch. He jumped off the fence, lifted up the fifth board, made a selection, and put on his boots.

Now with boots, hat, and bandana on, he jumped on the zebra. Sitting in the saddle he would take the reins, give them two pulls, and start riding to town to see if he could help anybody.

*   *   *

Making Trouble

There were three animals that disliked Yellow Dog. These three animals were cats that go by the names Midnight, Bandit, and Bright Eyes. Midnight was all black with yellow eyes, Bandit had off white fur with black markings around his bright, green, eyes, and Bright Eyes had light, brown, fur and bright blue eyes. They disliked Yellow Dog because of all the attention the town gave him. The three cats had been watching Yellow Dog since he came to town. They wanted the same attention he got, but they knew full well that a cat doesn't get the same attention as a dog. In truth, they didn't do anything to deserve the attention, but this didn't stop them from trying to ruin Yellow Dog's reputation.

Then they had a great idea. They thought if they spread terrible rumors about Yellow Dog, maybe people would get together and run him out of town. With Yellow Dog gone, they thought they would get all the attention.

So one evening, after Yellow Dog rode off into the sunset, back to his home, Bandit and Midnight walked softly into town ready to make trouble. When they got to the general store, they jumped up on the barrels that were outside. Mr. Jones who ran the store came out. Mr. Jones was startled to see them and said, "Hello Bandit, Hello Midnight, I didn't see you there." Then Bandit said,

"Well good evening Mr. Jones. Me and Midnight were just walking around quietly. Not like that certain yellow dog that I know."

That's when Mr. Jones said, "We are very lucky to have such a loyal and helpful dog."

Then Midnight said, "If I were you, I wouldn't be so friendly with that dog."

Surprised, Mr. Jones said, "Look, I know that cats and dogs don't get along, but what have you heard?"

Bandit then said "I heard that as soon as it's dark enough for everyone in town to be asleep, this dog comes back into town and steals food. He hides his tracks with fake cat paws over his own. He sneaks into people's houses, goes into their kitchens, and steals their food. No one hears him because of those fake cat paws."

Mr. Jones said, "That can't be true. He's too small to do that! He seems so nice!"

But that's when Midnight said, "I heard that he works for a con man." *(Note: a Con Man is a person who gets you into their confidence so that they can steal from you.)* "After he does services for you", Midnight continued, " he asks for excessive payment. He asks for more than he deserves. If you don't pay him he will bite you in the leg."

Then Mr. Jones said, "Believe me this dog is way too good to do stuff like that!"

After that Midnight and Bandit went to tell Bright Eyes that their lies weren't having the effect that they wanted. Bright Eyes just smiled and said "Don't worry, I bet you within a week they're all going to get together and run that dog out of town."

The next evening Bright Eyes visited Mr. Jones. When Mr. Jones saw Bright Eyes and said, "Hello", Bright Eyes said, "Listen Mr. Jones! I'm not sure about what Bandit and Midnight said but I know the real story. Yellow Dog is a spy from back East sent here to find out which stores in town might be going out of business. The ones

Yellow Dog finds out about will be shut down and then purchased."

When Mr. Jones heard this, he still didn't believe it, but it definitely gave him stuff to think about.

The next day Mrs. Smith came in to Mr. Jones store to buy new Sunday hats. Mr. Jones said, "Mrs. Smith, you know that dog who rides into town everyday to see if anybody needs him?"

"Of course I do, why?" said Mrs. Smith.

That's when Mr. Jones said, "Do you think he could be a spy sent here to buy out my store?" to which she said, "Of course not, why do you ask? He hardly seems like the spying type."

Then Mr. Jones said, "It was just something that the cat named Bright Eyes said to me last night."

Then she said "Now why would he do that? I thought he'd be too tired from coming into our houses to steal our food."

That's when Mr. Jones said "Who told you that?"

So Mrs. Smith said, " It was the cat named Bandit"

Just then Mr. Laden came in and said " I think you're both wrong, because I heard from the cat named Midnight that he works for some kind of con man and if you don't pay him, he bites you in the leg."

Just then Bob the butcher came in and said " Hello and how is everybody doing today?"

Then Mr. Laden, Mr. Jones, and Mrs. Smith all said, "Fine Bob just fine."

Then Bob said, " Now what's this I hear about that dog stealing food?"

So Mrs. Smith said "Well the cat named Bandit told me that as soon as it's dark enough for everyone to be asleep, the dog comes into town with a bag and steals their food from the kitchen, but we don't hear him because he wears fake cat paws so he can do it quietly."

Then Bob said "Don't be silly, he comes in to my shop and buys his food like everybody else in town."

But then Mr. Laden said "But what about what Midnight told me, about working for a con man? And what Bright Eyes told Mr. Jones about being a spy sent here to find out which stores in town might be going out of business?"

That's when Mr. Jones said, " Maybe we should ask him when he rides in."

*   *   *

Getting Started

As it turned out, the townspeople didn't have to wait very long for Yellow Dog to return. Soon they soon heard the sound of his horse's hoofs, and before long, Yellow Dog climbed down to the street and walked into the store. When he saw Mr. Laden, Bob the butcher, and Mrs. Smith in the store he said, " Hi and how are all of you doing this fine day?"

They all said " We're doing just fine."

Yellow Dog said "Great." Then he asked "Mr. Jones, do you happen to have any new cowboy hats?"

That's when Mr. Jones said " I sure do wait right here and I'll go and get them."

As Mr. Jones went to get the hats Yellow Dog said "So Mrs. Smith how's the family?" to which she answered "They're just fine thank you ."

That's when Mr. Jones came back with all of the cowboy hats and a mirror so the dog could see which ones he liked best. He then jumped up on to the counter and started trying on all of the hats. After a while he said, "O.K. Mr. Jones, I would like to take the white one, the black one, and the light blue one."

Mr. Jones said "O.K. and will someone come by later as always to pay?" to which the dog said "Of course."

Then Mr. Jones said "Good, and are you sure about the black one?"

Yellow Dog answered "Yes. It might help influence the people at my house."

Then Mr. Laden said "Why do you have people at your house? Are you working for a con man?"

The dog then got a look on his face that dogs get when they don't understand something they see. So Yellow Dog asked " What's a con man?"

Mr. Laden said "You mean to tell me that you work for one and you don't know?"

Still confused, the dog said, "Are you feeling alright, Mr. Laden? Maybe you should see a doctor."

Then Mr. Laden said "A con man is a person who does services, or promises people something when they only intend to steal their money. And I heard from the cat named Midnight that you work for one. That after you do these services, someday, when we least expect it, you're going to ask for payment, and if we don't pay you, you're going to bite us on the leg."

Then the dog got a shocked look on his face and said, "What? Are you kidding?! I would never do a thing like that. I do the services because it makes me happy to see you guys happy. And the people at my house— they are bullies, so I'm trying to teach them how bad it's going to be for them later on in life. In fact, I was thinking— if I wear the black hat with the black bandana, they will have more respect for me. Also dogs never believe what cats say about them."

Then Mr. Laden said "Listen, it's not that I don't believe you, but maybe I could come over to your house so I can see exactly what you mean."

The dog was then quiet while he scratched his left ear. Then he said "Sure, I'm headed back there right now." But before they left the store, Yellow Dog turned to Mr. Jones and said " How much for the hats?"

Mr. Jones started to add it up— "Let's see... each hat is $3.00, and you bought three, so that's three times three which is $9.00 all together."

They first went over to where Mr. Laden lived. Mr. Laden went to his stables and took out his horse named "Lighting." Then after he got on his horse, the dog asked the zebra nicely, as he always did, to kneel down so he could get on. After he was sitting on the saddle, Yellow Dog took the reins, gave them two firm tugs, and now rode off to his own house while Mr. Laden followed. When they got to his house, the dog told Mr. Laden to please wait for one minute as two people would be out soon to take care of the horses.

As they waited, Yellow Dog went up to the porch, pulled up the fifth floor board, and put the white and light blue hat into hat boxes. Then he took out the black bandana and then replaced the floor board. After that he asked Mr. Laden to tie the black bandana around his neck. So Mr. Laden got down off Lighting, told him to stay, and got down on his knees to tie the bandana around Yellow Dog's neck. Then the dog himself put on the black hat. He looked at himself in a piece of glass that he used as a mirror, and then took a quick look at Mr. Laden and asked how he looked.

Mr. Laden said "You look like a dog who needs to be taken seriously."

Then the dog said, " Good that's exactly what I was going for when I bought this black hat."

*   *   *

Helping Out

Yellow Dog gave four sharp high barks, and immediately three boys who looked about 16 or 17 years old came out of the house. They said "Yes sir ,what is it that you want us to do?" Yellow Dog gave the reins of Lighting and his zebra to two of the boys and jerked his head to the direction of the stables. The boys said "Yes sir, right away sir."

The boys took the reins and led both horses to the stables. As they led the horses away, the dog led the third boy back to the house and gave him one high bark which told him to stay where he was until he retuned. When Yellow Dog got back, he had the money and a note which the boy was to show Mr. Jones. When the boy saw the note he knew exactly what to do. Then the dog went back to the stables and saw the boys coming out.

When they saw the dog they went over to where he was and said "We gave both of them plenty of food and water. Is that all sir?" But the dog thought he'd go and check anyway, so he gave two long howls and a short bark to each of the boys which told them to stay where they were until he came back from checking. When he finally came back, he yipped and wagged his tail which meant that the boys did a good job. So after that the boys said," Thank you sir." And then he nudged them back in the house.

After they were back in the house Mr. Laden said "I still don't get it." So the dog explained, "People bully others for lots of reasons. For some it's insecurity, for others it's because if they're scared of something silly, but they don't want anybody to find out about it, so they act cool and mean like they don't even know the meaning of honest work. For some of them, I try to figure out what they're afraid of and show them what they think is scary is not always true. And still, to others, like the two that took care of the horses, they find out that work can also be fun if you enjoy doing it. They find they can get praise if they do it well, and also that people get angry if you don't do it well."

Just then, the dog noticed that the roof was not painted. He told Mr. Laden to be quiet and to watch closely. The dog then gave two loud barks and, this time, a boy and a girl came out. The boy was about 15 years old and the girl was about 16. When they went over to the dog, they said "Yes sir, what is it that you want us to do?" Then the dog did three long howls and pointed to the roof . That's when the boy and the girl both exchanged looks of worry.

"Listen sir," said the girl, "we can explain. We were going to do the roof, but we couldn't find the ladders." Then the dog looked at the boy who said "It's true sir. We both looked." So the dog went to the stables and came out with two pieces of rope. Then he whispered to Mr. Laden to tie one rope around the waist of the boy and the other around the waist of the girl, then hand him the other ends. After Mr Laden did that, the dog led the boy and girl to the back of the house.

When they got there, he led them to a tool shed where they saw two ladders. Upon seeing the ladders, the boy and girl promised the dog they would get started on the roof, bright and early the next morning. Then the dog chewed through the rope and nudged them back in the house.

By this time, the boy that he had sent to pay for the hats had come back. When he saw the dog, he went over to him and said "Everything is taken care of sir." Then all the dog did was nod his head to let the boy know he did a good job, then nudged him back into the house.

After all was said and done, Mr. Laden had no choice but to remark "Well that's pretty impressive, and I get precisely what you're saying."

Then the dog replied "Good. I'm glad that you do. So what else did those cats say about me?"

Mr. Laden told him "One of them said that you steal our food", but I know that's not true, because Bob the butcher told me, Mrs. Smith, and Mr. Jones that you go into his store and buy your food like everybody else."

Mr. Laden continued "and the other one said you're a spy from back east, sent here to find out which stores in town might be going out of business."

The dog chuckled and assured him "Believe me, I'm not a spy, and I don't work for a con man; plus, if I buy my own food, why would I steal? So do you believe me?"

Mr. Laden smiled, "Of course I do." Then he noticed the time. "Well it's getting late, so I'd better say good bye." Then without another word, he went into the stables, and a moment later, he re-appeared with Lightning. Mr. Laden waved good bye to the dog as he and Lightning rode back to his house.

The dog then walked back to his house to have dinner and get some sleep. The next morning, after Yellow Dog woke up and had breakfast, he went to his mailbox (which was lower than most so he could easily get the mail). When he opened the mailbox he found an invitation which said that he was the guest of honor at Mr. Mitchell's farm. It didn't say why, so the first thing he did was go over to the porch. He lifted up the fifth floor board, and took out the light blue hat and bandana, so he could wear them that evening. Then he replaced the floor board and put the hat and bandana behind the mirror so they wouldn't get too dirty. He then went to the door of the house and barked three times before letting out a long howl, which meant he wanted everybody out of the house, on the double, and not to keep him waiting.

Within moments, he heard the sound of doors slamming and sneakers running as all of the boys and girls ran out of the house as if it were on fire. After everybody was gone, the dog gave three sharp barks, and they all stood at attention. Then the dog gave the invitation to a

boy about 14 years old. He gave him a single bark which

meant he was to read it out loud. After he did that, he said

"But we've never spent a night alone without you before

sir. What if some of us feel the urge to start bullying

again?"

Then the dog went to the house, opened the door,

and went in. When he retuned he had a photo album. He

gave two quick barks which meant everybody should sit

down and wait. Then the dog started flipping through the

album. When he came across a picture of Mr. Laden, he

took it out of the album and showed it all around. When it

got to the boys who took care of the horses one of them

said "Permission to speak, sir?" The dog nodded his head

yes and the boy who was16 said "This is the guy you rode

up with yesterday. Is he going to stay with us until you come home sir?"

The dog nodded his head *yes* again, then he nudged everybody back inside the house except for the one boy and girl who went to the back of the house to get started on the roof . After Yellow Dog was certain they were doing the roof, he barked once then howled twice. Then a boy about 16 years old came out and said "Yes sir, what is it?"

The dog led the boy to the porch. He lifted the floor board and when the boy saw all of the stuff, he said "Is all this stuff yours, sir?" Yellow Dog nodded his head *yes,* then pointed to the white hat and bandana. The boy looked at the dog and asked "You want me to put the white hat and bandana on you, right sir?" The dog then yipped and wagged his tail, and the boy said "Yes sir, right away sir."

After taking out the white hat and bandana to match, the boy put the hat on the dog's head. Then he kneeled down to tie the bandana around his neck. The dog took a quick look at himself and was very pleased. The dog then nudged him back into the house. Yellow Dog went to the back of the house to see how the boy and girl were doing on the roof. When the girl and boy saw the dog out of the corner of their eyes, they stopped what they were doing and came down the ladders. The boy said "So what do think so far, sir?" The dog went to take a look, cocked his head to one side, then went over to the boy and girl and barked once and wagged his tail which meant that they were doing a good job. They said "Thank you so very much sir. We'll just go finish up now, and thanks again sir."

After they went back to work, the dog went to the stables to get on his zebra and head off to town to see if Mr. Laden could, in fact, stay with them until he got home from Mr. Mitchell's farm. When he got to Mr. Laden's house, he scratched at the door to go inside. But when the door opened, it wasn't Mr. Laden but his son Jackson. At first Jackson didn't see anyone. But when he looked down and saw it was Yellow Dog, he said "Hello and how are you today?"

The dog answered, "I'm doing just fine, but who are you?"

So Jackson continued "Why I'm Jackson, Mr. Laden's son, and listen, I know that they say you're the most loyal dog ever, always ready to help, but I was wondering do you really not have a name?"

Then the dog shrugged "No, I don't have a name because I was abandoned after I was born, so with seven brothers and eight sisters, my mom didn't have time to give all of us names."

Then Jackson said "Really that's too bad. How about I give you one? Would you like that?"

The dog said "Yes I would like that very much." So Jackson looked very closely and all around Yellow Dog to see if he could find a perfect name. After looking he said "You know my dad told me what you do for the bullies at your house, so how about a good name, but also a tough name, like Rex? Do you like the name Rex?"

That's when the dog scratched his ear while he thought about it. Then he said excitedly, "Rex! I like it so much, this evening I'll announce to everyone that my

name is Rex." So after getting back on his zebra, he went

into town to see if he could find Mr. Laden. But what he

didn't know is that those three cats were quietly following

him.

*   *   *

What To Do?

When Yellow Dog found Mr. Laden, he was at the blacksmith getting new horse shoes made for Lighting. So when he walked in, and when Mr. Laden saw him, he said "Well hello and how are you today?"

Yellow Dog was, of course, doing fantastic and was excited to tell Mr. Laden why. "Oh I'm feeling just great. After so many years of not having what I wanted most of all— which was a name— I am proud to announce that thanks to your son Jackson, I have just that now." The he continued to Mr. Laden, with a big smile and said "I have a name and my name is Rex."

Then Mr. Laden and the blacksmith whose name was Dave said "Wow that was some speech", to which Mr. Laden added " Yes you should say that at the party tonight."

The dog was surprised and asked "What party?"

Then Mr. Laden realized his mistake "Oh no, I shouldn't have said that, it was to be a surprise for you later, now it's spoiled!"

Then the dog said, "Listen maybe it can still be saved. I'll pretend like I didn't hear what you just said which is going to be hard because I do have a very good hearing, I hear better than humans." So tonight I'll pretend to be so surprised that no one including Mr. Mitchell will know that I knew about it."

That's when Dave said "Are you sure it will work?"

That's when Rex said "Believe me, I've been around a long time, it always works."

Then the blacksmith said, "Okay, so what brings you here?" Then Rex said, "Well I wanted to ask Mr. Laden a question and when he wasn't at home I thought he might be in town somewhere and here he is."

Mr. Laden then asked "Okay, so what's your question?"

So the Dog told him "Remember when I showed you how I deal with bullies? Well this is the first time that I am leaving them alone, so I need someone to keep an eye on them until I come back and I was wondering if you could do it?"

Mr. Laden explained truthfully, "Well I would rather be at your party tonight, but as a favor to you, I'll do it."

That's when the dog said "Thank you very much for saying that you can stay with them."

But just as Dave was about to leave he said "Wait a minute I would like to make you a collar and name tag, free of charge, if you want one."

Rex, of course, said "Yes I would like that very much", and with that, Dave went to work making a name tag for him. When he was finished with the name tag, he attached it to a leather collar then bent down and put it on him.

The cats thought that this was strange but that it just might work. After leaving town, Yellow Dog— Rex— went back to Mr. Laden's house to show Jackson his new nametag and collar. When he got there he scratched at the door again, and just as before, Jackson opened the door. When he looked down he was surprised to see Yellow Dog back at his house again. He asked "Hey what are you

doing back here?"

Then the dog said " I just wanted to show you this

new collar and nametag that Dave the blacksmith made for

me, and to tell you that your dad is staying at my house

tonight. So he can keep an eye on the bullies until I come

home."

Then Jackson said "Well it's a very nice collar and

nametag and I was wondering something myself: Since

you never did any normal dog stuff, would like to try

playing ball?"

Rex said "Sure why not." Now when the cats saw

this, they knew that if they could convince the whole town

that the dog really belonged to Mr. Laden's son before that

evening, in no time at all, they could run him out of town .

They set off to work, and because they knew that this was

a small town, they only had to tell one person and that

person was Mr. Jones. Now Mr. Jones couldn't believe it

when they told him, but when he saw Rex and Jackson

playing ball he knew that those cats were telling the truth

this time.

*   *   *

The First Step

News of what Mr. Jones saw spread like wild fire, and soon everybody in town was talking— from Bob the butcher to the hired hands at Mr. Mitchell's farm who were setting up for the party. With the news, the workers at the farm were told to stop working as the party was canceled due to the rumors about Western Dog belonging to Mr. Laden and his son Jackson.

They all wondered what to do, until Bright Eyes said "I say we band together and run him out of town." Some thought that was a good idea, but most people thought *what good would that do?* That Yellow Dog would just go to another town and hook up with another family and do it again. He had to learn that it wasn't nice to fool people. So they talked about it and suggested putting him in the stocks or in jail. Most people thought stocks wouldn't work because he's too small, so jail was the only option. But now the problem was how to do it so fast that it will make his head spin.

Soon the sheriff said "Leave it to me. I'll go with Mr. Laden to his house and tell him that I'm his escort to the party, but that first I want him to look at something in my office. Then when we get there I'll tell him to walk into the first cell then— Bang! I close the door and lock it." The sheriff got more excited as he went into details on his plan. "Then I'll press a special button and shackles will come out and go around his paws and neck and lock themselves so he knows what happens when people break the law."

Some people thought the shackle around the neck was a little harsh, so the sheriff promised to leave out that part unless he made an outburst. That evening, after Mr.

Laden had arrived at the dog's house, a girl about 13 years

old was just tying the light blue bandana around the dog's

neck. The dog looked at himself, then back to the girl and

yipped once and wagged his tail.

The girl then said "Thank you sir." Then he nudged

her back inside the house. When he saw Mr. Laden he said

"Great, you're here. There's a list on the living room table

of what to do in case anything happens while I'm at the

party." Then it occurred to him to also ask "And, how do I

look?"

Mr. Laden told him "You look very nice." Just then

the sheriff, whose name was Al, came over and said

"Hello, so I see you have a name now, it's Rex right?" to

which the dog said "Yes and why are you here?"

Al explained "Well I thought you would like an escort to the party."

The dog said "Okay, but since it's such a cool evening, I think we should walk." So they started off down the road. After a while Al said "You know before we go to the party, I want to show you something in my office, please come with me."

Rex, thought about it and said "But I don't want to be late for my party"— but Al assured him "Oh, this won't take long."

They went into the Sheriff's station, and the dog said "Do you mind if I take off my boots, hat, and bandana for a little while, just in case this thing you want me to see is dirty?"

Al said "Not at all, go ahead." So Yellow Dog took off his boots, hat, and bandana. Then Al put the hat and bandana on a hook and put the boots on the floor under the

hook but out of way, so no one would trip. Then Yellow

Dog said "So what is this thing that you want me to see?"

And that's when Al said "It's right over here… in this

first cell."

*   *   *

Nightmare Fright

So after the dog walked in, and while he had his back turned, Al shut the door and locked it. When Yellow Dog turned around to the sound of the door slamming, he didn't have time to ask why, because as soon as Al locked the door, he pressed a button on his desk. Suddenly four sets of shackles came out of the walls, and even though Yellow Dog tried to get away from them, they soon went around his legs and locked themselves.

That's when the dog said "Hey what is the meaning of all this?" to which Al said "Why didn't you tell us you belonged to Mr. Laden and Jackson?"

Rex said "What are you talking about? I don't belong to Jackson or Mr. Laden. I live the way my wild relations the wolf and coyotes do— alone without a pack!"

But Al said, "Sorry, but I don't believe you. Besides we have a witness." The dog seemed confused but Al continued "Mr. Jones— he saw you playing ball with Jackson earlier today, now if that's not the way a boy plays ball with his dog I don't know what is."

That's when Yellow Dog said "Well what about my party?"

Al said, " As of right now your party is called off, because we can't hold a party for somebody who lies to us." After this, Yellow Dog didn't know what to say. How could Mr. Jones have thought that him playing ball with Jackson meant he belonged to him. Unless someone saw him, then told Mr. Jones.

So he said "Al did anyone tell Mr. Jones that I was playing ball with Jackson?"

Then Al said, "Ah-ha, so you admit that you were playing ball with Jackson!"

That's when Rex said, "Yes, I did, but who told him?"

Al admitted "Well Mr. Jones did say that three cats that go by the names of Midnight, Bright Eyes, and Bandit told him that they saw you at the blacksmith shop getting that collar and nametag then you went back to Mr. Laden's house."

Then Rex said "You mean to say that those cats told Mr. Jones about me playing ball, and they thought that meant that I belong to Mr. Laden and Jackson?"

Al smiled and said "Exactly."

Then Rex said, "Listen Al, this is all a big misunderstanding. I would never keep a secret from anyone in this town, and also, cats always lie. That's why dogs never believe what cats say about them."

Al still was unconvinced— "But how about Mr. Jones? Do you believe him?"

The dog said "Sure but he could have asked me instead of listening to those cats. If you want my opinion, those cats should be the ones in here, not me."

Al asked "On what grounds?"

Then Rex said "Oh right, I forgot you need grounds for an arrest, right?"

Al admitted "Right, but listen— it's getting late but— I'm warning you— one more outburst from you and I'll be forced to put a shackle around your neck, so I'm going to say goodnight now."

But the dog wasn't giving up so he said "Really you're making a big mistake." But right after he said that, there was a shackle around his neck just like Al said there would be if there was one more outburst. By this time Yellow Dog was very upset, but there wasn't anything else that he could do right now. So after Al had left he took a pillow and blanket from one of the beds that was in the cell, put them on the floor, and went under the blanket until he came out the other end.

Yellow Dog put his head on the pillow and cried himself to sleep wondering why Mr. Jones listened to Bandit, Midnight, and Bright Eyes, and why did he not just ask him why he was at Mr. Laden's house playing ball with Jackson instead of jumping to the wrong conclusions.

Later that evening he had the most horrible, terrifying, scariest nightmare a dog could ever have (well a dog that's in a position that this dog was in, at any rate.) I mean picture this, you're in jail with shackles around your legs and neck for something that you know you didn't do. But just because one person saw you doing whatever it was, then listened to animals who always lie, then jumped to the wrong conclusions and now everybody in town thinks it was you.

In the nightmare he's being carted off to a special prison just for dogs. Where the dogs are stripped of their collars. Fitted with black and white striped hats and shirts. Then given numbers instead of their names. They stay there until they die or until they are ready to be good dogs. So once he's there they take off his collar but then he says "Hey wait a minute. What are you doing with my collar?"

Then the Dalmatian who's name is Danny said, "You don't need a collar anymore, here we give you a number. So here you'll be known as prisoner number 17. Now I'm going to lead you to your cell. Then tomorrow you're going to see how we deal with bad dogs like you."

So with a chain around his neck he's lead to a cell with his number on the top. Gets pushed in and then chained to the wall. After the Dalmatian left he howls so loud that the rest of the dogs that were near him didn't know why he was howling. So they started to howl as well. But then two tough Bulldogs and four Great Danes came out and said "Everybody stop all that howling or else."

At that very minute everybody did stop because unlike the yellow dog who was new, the other dogs knew what the *"or else"* meant. After the Bulldogs and Great Danes left, the dog in the cell next to him said "Hey number 17 what did they get you for?" Yellow Dog turned to see a Jack Russell terrier looking at him, then he said "Who are you?" to which he answered "I'm prisoner number 18, what did they get you for?"

Yellow Dog said "Lying about not belonging to anybody... but I say that it was all a big mistake." Then prisoner number 18 (who's name used to be Jeff) said "That's the first time I've ever heard that one, I'm here because I dig a little too much."

Rex then said "Well that's not so bad. I mean, what do they expect sometimes, when we have to dig we dig."

That's when number 18 said "Yeah digging a little or when you're trying to bury something. But digging in the park, at school, a forest replanting project, the fire station and burying stuff you shouldn't like car keys, stuffed animals, new ones from the store, homework, and new shoes."

Rex was thinking "Boy, he really does have a problem" when suddenly prisoner number 20 called out " You think he's got problems, mine are worse." Then they both turned to see a very lovely, young French poodle who used to be called Princess. So Yellow Dog said "Well let's hear it", and prisoner number 20 said "I'm in here because I can't stand going to the dog stylists. Yes I know what you're thinking— what dog does, but I really act up so my owners didn't know what else to do. So they called up this place and sent me here."

Then Yellow Dog said, "What about obedience school?"

Number 18 admitted "Got kicked out of every single one, because of the digging."

Number 20 said "Looked like I was something a cat dragged in." A few minutes later a Cocker Spaniel came out and said "O.K. no more talking, time for everybody to go to sleep. Lock it down." Then after all of the lights were out she went over to Rex's cell and said "Now tomorrow we'll find out what you're good at doing and then you'll do that until we think you've seen how bad it is when dogs break the law."

The next morning the prisoners were waking up, then led to a place where they all ate together. Today it was bread and water, just like what they give prisoners in movies and books. Then it was time for them to work, and time for the yellow dog to see how they handled bad dogs. As all of the other dogs were led to a yard, Yellow Dog was led inside where he was fitted with a black and white striped hat and shirt like the other dogs to show that he was a prisoner. Then he was led out to the yard where he saw dogs chained to carts waiting to be loaded up with stones dug out by other dogs. Dogs who were washing the black and white striped hats and shits on washboards. Dogs who had their front paws locked into special peddles so they can make license plates and other things.

Yellow Dog was then chained to a cart when he heard a Bulldog say "Now you wait here until your cart is full of stones, then you pull it over to the other side of the yard. You unload, then you come back here for more, and do it again, got it?"

All he could do was nod his head *yes*. After the Bulldog left, he heard digging behind him and saw that the sound came from prisoner number 18, who he had met last night; but when he tried to talk to him, one of the Great Danes who told all of the dogs to stop howling said "No talking to other prisoners while they're working, now get going." That's when the dog noticed his cart was full, so with all his might he pulled the cart across the yard. When he got to the other side he got unchained, then pulled the back of the cart down. With his nose he then rolled the big ones onto a conveyer belt, and lastly with his paws, put the small ones into pails, and then the Bulldogs take it from there.

After that was done, he went back to the cart and put the ramp back up. Then he went to the front, got chained up again, and went back to the other side of the yard to get more stones. But after three hours he was getting tired; but if he tried to lie down, a Great Dane would say "Oh no you don't, no one rests until their work is done." So after another four hours, five Great Danes and three Bulldogs came out and said "O.K. it's time for lunch."

At first Yellow Dog was happy to have a break and something to eat and drink, but he was disappointed when he found out it was bread and water again. After lunch it was time to switch jobs. So this time the dog was led to a place where his front paws were locked into special pedals so he can make license plates. But after the Bulldog that had put him there had left he didn't know why if number 18's problem was digging- why did they have him do it in the first place. When he looked around at the other dogs they all looked kind of strange. I mean no one looked happy— who would be? But still, they looked like they knew what they had to do and they also looked like they didn't even remember having a name because here they were all given numbers.

When it was time for dinner, Yellow Dog was not surprised to see that it was bread and water. But before leading them back to their cells, Danny the Dalmatian, who takes off the collars, said "O.K. before we take you back to your cells, who has to use the bathroom?" Then a few dogs including the yellow dog barked then Danny said "O.K. follow me."

He led them to a spot where they could do what they had to do, then they were led back inside. After everybody was pushed in and chained to the wall for the night, Yellow Dog said "Hey number 18 are you up?"

Number 18 said "Yeah, what's up?"

Then Rex said "Why do they have you digging. I thought that digging was why you were sent here in the first place?"

Then the Jack Russell terrier said "Well maybe if I dig because I'm supposed to, maybe I'll get it out of my system and can go home to be a good dog."

Then the little yellow dog said "Well I have another question?"

"Shoot", said number 18.

That's when Rex said "Why do the other dogs look like they're in some kind of trance or under hypnosis?"

Then the Jack Russell terrier said "That's the method they use here, they break you down until you obey their command, learn to respond to your number, until you learn to be a good dog or if you're old until you die."

*   *   *

Getting Ready

Soon it was morning, and he woke up from his nightmare. At first he was relieved that he was back in the town. But then he realized that he still had shackles around his legs and neck. Just then Mr. Laden came in and he was followed by every boy and girl that was in the dog's house. When he saw all of them he whispered to Mr. Laden "What are they all doing here?"

Then Mr. Laden said "When you weren't home, they got really nervous, and the word around town by cats that go by the names of Bandit, Midnight, and Bright Eyes, says that you were here. At first I didn't believe it because you said cats always lie about what they say about dogs, and yet here you are."

*   *   *

Getting the Proof

One of the boys from the house asked "Why didn't you tell us sir?" But Yellow Dog didn't know what to say. Sure he could bark, howl, and do gestures but there was a lot to say, and he didn't know how to do it in a way people would understand. So even though he knew it was going to be a shock to them, when he would show them that he could speak human.

So he said "O.K. here's what happened, and yes I can speak human. I never had a name because I was abandoned after I was born and with seven brothers and eight sisters my mom didn't have time to name us all. So I was going to Mr. Laden's house to see if he could stay with you guys, but when I scratched at the door, his son Jackson answered and let me in. Jackson even gave me a name which by the way is Rex. Then I went into town and found Mr. Laden at the blacksmith's shop getting new shoes for his horse. So after announcing my name to Mr. Laden and the blacksmith, he asked me if I would like a collar and nametag free of charge, so I thought what was the harm in that. And then I went back to Mr. Laden's house to show Jackson."

Then Mr. Laden said "Should I tell them the rest?"

The dog said "Sure, I could actually use some water, because that was a mouthful for a little dog like me."

So since they knew it was okay, one of the girls went with Mr. Laden back to the dog's house to get him a bowl of water. A few minutes later they returned with a bowl of water. After, Al opened the cell door for a minute, so they could give him the water. Then after re-locking the cell after the girl and Mr. Laden went out, Mr. Laden said, " I was told by my son that he thought that Rex might like to try playing ball since he never got the chance but that was it."

That's when one of the boys said "So I guess that means there was no party last night, right sir?" Then all the dog could do was sadly nod his head.

That's when one of the girls said "Sir, if we find out how those cats found out where you were going yesterday and prove your innocence, plus get them to confess, maybe if the party goes back on, can we go?" Then he thought about it while scratching his ear, which was a little hard because of the shackles; then he said "Sure why not?" So off they went to see if they could find out how those cats found out where he was yesterday.

First they decided to start at the house and retrace the dog's steps. For the first few hours they didn't see a thing, but then a girl about 13 years old called all of the other boys and girls over to where she was. When they all got to the stables the girl said "Hey look at what I found here in the dirt." They all looked and next to the zebra's foot prints were cat paw prints.

Then the girl said "Who has a camera?"

Then a boy about 18 years old said "I do, and I get exactly what you're saying, but we also need a magnifying glass because those cat prints are pretty small." So after taking a picture of the paw prints and stable to show the dog where they saw them. They followed them and saw that they went to Mr. Laden's house, then into town leading to the blacksmith's shop (where they found three cat hairs), then back to Mr. Laden's house. Afterwards the boys and girls went back to the sheriff's office to go and show Rex what they had found. But when they came in, he was asleep, so they decided to come back tomorrow.

That night he had the nightmare again, and this time he knew they might try him on washing the black and white striped shirts and hats. Then came a surprise, during lunch Danny the Dalmatian said, "Okay everybody, listen up. We have an announcement. One of the dogs has learned to be a good dog." Everyone looked up to see who he was talking out it. "So now we can give the French poodle back her collar and her name which happens to be *Princess*. Her owners are right outside, and they'll be happy to have her back."

The other dogs were happy for her and hoped that some day soon they would be reunited with their owners. After lunch, Yellow Dog found out that he was right, because he was led to a place where a German Shepard and a Labrador were washing the black and white hats on washboards. After seeing what he had to do, without even saying Hi, he just did what the other dogs were doing. When no one was looking, he looked over at the other side of the yard and saw another thing that they had the prisoners do.

Lying down in two lawn chairs were two Bulldogs and next to them there was one Dalmatian and one Jack Russell terrier /Dalmatian mixed breed fanning them with big feathery fans. Soon it was morning again and Yellow Dog was just waking up. Relieved that he was back in the town again. Sad because he was still in jail and still had the shackles on him, and wondered what was going to happen.

Suddenly there was a knock on the door of the sheriff's office. When Al went to open it, three of the girls and four of the boys were on the other side of the door. They asked Al if they could talk to the dog, and he said"Sure", so they went over to the cell. The girl who found the cat paw prints and the boy who found the three cat hairs in the blacksmith's shop went over and said "Sir after we left yesterday, we went straight to work trying to find anything that would tell us how those cats found out where you went yesterday."

The girl took a breath then continued "and this is what we found out. According to the paw prints, they were hiding behind the barn until you came out on your zebra; then they followed you to Mr. Laden's place where they hid behind some bushes, and then into the blacksmith shop where we found these three cat hairs and saw you get that collar and name tag. And finally, they followed you back

to Mr. Laden's place."

That's when the dog said "Well that's a pretty good

start. Listen, why don't you all go back home and see what

else you can do." Then he added "don't worry everything

will turn out fine and I'll be able to come home

soon." (Though, in truth, he wasn't quite sure if he'd ever

be free again).

       *.   *   *

Making a Plan

As the kids were leaving, one of them said to Yellow Dog "Sir you know that nightmare you've been having? I was thinking maybe it's because you're nervous. Maybe if I stayed with you tonight to keep you calm and maybe hold your paw or rub your back— then maybe you won't have the nightmare."

Rex thought about it and said "That sounds like a great idea. Why don't you go and ask Al if it's okay for you to stay the night. And tell him why. Then if he says *yes,* ask him to tell you a time to come back here. And then you'll tell the rest of the boys and girls afterwards.

So off she went to ask Al if it was okay, and he said that it was. She then asked him what time she should come back and he said "around 6:00 pm" because that's when he goes to sleep." After leaving the sheriff's office the girl told the dog that Al said it was okay for her to stay for just one night.

Later that evening, at about 5:30 pm, the girl went to the sheriff's office with a sleeping bag and pillow. She slept just outside the dog's jail cell and put her hand through the bars— holding his paw and rubbing his back to keep him calm and relaxed, hoping he wouldn't have the nightmare again. But it didn't work. It not only happened again, but it was even worse. This time they had him washing the clothes on the washboards.

In the afternoon they had him chained to a cart to pull stones across the yard. Then in the evening they had him fanning one the Bulldogs with a big feathery fan, and he couldn't seem to do that very well. Then the Bulldog got angry and said "No that's too fast", and when he would slow down, the Bulldog would say "No, now it's too slow." Soon it was morning, and he woke up the way he always did after having the nightmare— relieved to be back in the town, but sad that he was shackled by his legs and neck.

After the girl woke up, she asked him if having somebody there to keep him relaxed worked. But the dog's answer was of course "No" because it had happened again." Then the girl said "Oh, I'm sorry sir, I thought it would help."

He then said "Well it was a nice idea, anyway." But as the girl was leaving, she handed something to the sheriff; you see, before she left to go to the sheriff's office, one of the boys asked her to take the photos that he took, so he could take a look. Later that same day he wondered how he was going to get those cats to confess. Then Al went over to him and said, "Rex, you know how I said I didn't believe you before?"

Rex answered "Yeah so?"

To which Al said "Well just before the girl who spent the night here left, she handed me the pictures the boys showed you, and now that I've seen them, I've changed my mind and I do believe you."

That's when Rex said "Really? That's great, so how's about getting these shackles off and letting me go?"

But Al said "Wait, I got an idea. I have a feeling that those cats might want you out of the way for some reason, but I'm not sure why?"

But just then the dog's nose started twitching. Then he got a strong whiff of something that sent a message to his brain and then he said "You know what Al, I know exactly what it is and I have a way that we can get them to tell us what it is— without them knowing. Now I know that you hang people for crimes, do you think it would work for me?"

So Al thought about it and said "You mean, let the word get around town that we are going to hang you, and make sure the cats know; so before we hang you by the neck until you are dead, they will come forward and confess whatever it is that they did?"

The dog said "Exactly. It's fool-proof, it can't fail."

Al agreed, "I think it's a pretty good idea, but the problem is we don't have a gallows here. If we ever need the gallows, should we have to hang anybody, we have to go to the next town over and borrow theirs."

Yellow Dog then asked "How long does it take to get the gallows from there to here?"

"A day or two", said Al. Then there was a silence while Yellow Dog scratched his ear again— which he had bit of trouble doing since there were shackles around his legs.

Then he thought out the plan further "I think the next thing to do is— to get two people to go and get the gallows, then my people can help get the word out around town that I am going to be hanged. The key is to make sure those cats hear it."

That's when Al said "Okay. How about we get Mr. Laden and Mr. Smith?"

Rex agreed immediately "If you tell them the plan, it will be perfect." Then Rex added "But before you go, could you call my house and tell all of the boys and girls to come here? This way they can get the word out."

"Sure, what's your number?" Saw Al.

And Rex then responded "It's 663-4695."

Al called the number at the dog's house. The boys and girls were ready to do anything Rex asked. They heard the telephone ring, and one of the girls went to answer it. After she said "*Hello*", a voice said "Hello, this is Al, the sheriff. The dog says that he needs your help, and he wants you to come right over."

The girl perked up and told the sheriff "We'll be right over."

She hung up the phone and went to tell the girls and boys what the sheriff had said. When they got to the sheriff's office, the dog told them what was going to happen, and what he needed them to do. Then Al left to find Mr. Smith and Mr. Laden. When he found them, he asked if they would go to the next town over and get the gallows, and when they returned, he would fill them in on the plan.

Mr. Laden got on his horse Lighting and Mr. Smith got in his flatbed truck, and they both went to the next town to borrow their gallows. When they got to the next town, they went directly to that town's Sheriff— Sheriff Matthew. They asked Matthew if they could borrow their gallows for a short while. Without asking any questions, Matthew said "Why of course you can" and he even helped get it on to the flatbed truck. Once they got the gallows on the truck, Mr. Smith and Mr. Laden drove back to town very carefully so as not to destroy the gallows.

When they got back, they told Al that they have the gallows. It was time to get the word around town that they were going to hang that dog at high noon tomorrow. When

Al told the dog the good news, the dog relayed the message to all of the boys and girls. As they were leaving one of the boys seemed confused "Sir", he said, "why do we have to do it at high noon?"

Rex said "Because that's when they always do it on TV and in the movies. I guess you could say it's a tradition. Now get going. We got to make sure those cats hear about this."

Then the boy said "Right away, sir."

So they went through the town telling everybody they saw that tomorrow they were going to hang that dog. When they came to Mr. Jones' store, they saw Bright Eyes, Midnight, and Bandit snoozing in patches of sun. At first they wondered how they were going to get the cats to know if they were asleep; then one of the boys said "I've got it, it's so simple, yet so perfect."

The rest of them asked "What is so simple, yet so perfect?" The boy explained "first we need to wake them up, so some of you will have to pretend to cry and make sure you do it nice and loud so it will be sure to get them up; then we will tell them exactly what Yellow Dog told us to say, and see what happens."

Then all eight girls started to cry, nice and loud too, while some of the guys tried to calm them down. When the cats woke up, Midnight said "What's wrong with them? Why are they so upset?"

Some of the other boys then said "Didn't you hear the news? Tomorrow at high noon they're going to hang that yellow dog for lying to us about not belonging to anybody, and…well… it's just that we're going to miss him, because he's helped us so much."

The cats couldn't believe it, all they wanted was a little attention and now the dog was to be hanged. That's when Bandit said "Okay, this has gone way out of proportion. We need to stop it."

Midnight said "But how? They already decided that they are going to hang him."

Bandit told him "Listen, before some gets hanged, they always give him one last chance to be saved. So when the sheriff says "Is there anyone here who would like to come forward to save the life of this dog please step forward now, we step forward and explain everything."

The other two were not so sure, but they knew it wasn't supposed to go this far. They had all decided that tomorrow they will tell everybody the whole story and save the dog's life.

All too soon it was time to carry out the dog's plan, so Al woke Rex up and said "Well here it is the day we find out if the cats come forward or not. Are you sure about this?"

Rex answered "Like I said, it's fool proof. See, though we don't get along, we also can't stand to see each other in pain." Then Al took the shackles off his legs and neck, and he was then led out to the gallows to be put in a hangman's noose and read his last rights.

Al went up to Yellow Dog, put the rope around his neck, and said, loud enough for the crowd to hear, "Rex today you are going to be hanged for lying to this town of not belonging to anybody. We will ask you now, how do you plead?"

Rex answered "Not Guilty."

Then Al said "I see you say that you are not guilty, and yet when asked if you were playing ball with Jackson the other day, you admitted that you were." Al paused and then continued his speech "Now I'm not saying that playing ball is a crime, but why would a dog who doesn't belong to anybody, go and play ball anyway?"

That's when Rex said, "Oh I don't know maybe because *it's fun.*"

Al said, "I see. And do you think it's fun to lie?"

The dog said, "No but I didn't lie, I always tell the truth."

"Really?" Said Al, "well I don't think this town believes that you did. They believe that you lied and for that we have decided to hang you."

*   *   *

The Party

The dog did his best to plead his case: "But what about the bullies at my house? They need me. I help them so much."

Then a chorus of voices came from the boys and girls saying "Don't worry sir, we will remember everything that you taught us, and with your permission sir we would like to teach it to others."

Then the dog said "You have my permission, just remember the motto: 'Teasing Is Never Pleasing.'"

Then Al said, "Now if there is anyone here who has reason why this dog should not be hanged, let him or her step forward now." A long pause followed. And that's when Midnight, Bright Eyes, and Bandit stepped forward. Midnight said "Stop! This dog is telling the truth. He does not belong to anybody. It was me, Bright Eyes, and Bandit we spread terrible rumors about him, because we were jealous of all the attention he was getting and we wanted some attention too." Then Bandit added "So we thought that maybe if you thought the dog lied you would run him out of town, and we would get all of the attention. But we never meant for to go this far."

That's when Bright Eyes said "It's true, so I say, if anyone should be in a hangman's noose, it should us, not the dog."

Then Rex gave a look to Al and all of the boys and girls. Then he turned back to the cats and said "Thanks for coming forward."

*　　　*　　　*

Make it look Real

"Okay, Al. Let me loose."

As Yellow Dog was set free, Bandit, Bright Eyes and Midnight said "So you planned the whole thing?" to which the dog said, "Yeah everything, just to see if you would come forth and confess. And you did, but I sort of knew that you would, because even though we don't get along, we can't stand to see the other one in pain."

Then Bandit said, "But what are we supposed to do, I mean how do you get all of this attention?"

That's when Rex said, "I get it because I help people in the town just by being there when they need me, just like any other dog."

Then Midnight said "Do you we could do that too?"

"As a matter of fact *Yes*, he said, "because I've noticed that most of the houses have a bit of a rodent problem. Now I can't do anything about that, because I am a dog, not a cat like you three; but maybe you could help by doing what cats do best which is catch mice and rats. I bet that will get you the right kind of attention, just like I got." In truth, all three cats thought it was a good idea to try, so they asked if there were places they could start, and he knew of three such places.

First they went to the house of Mr. and Mrs. Smith, and when the dog scratched at the door, Mr. Smith said, "Hi how are you?"

Rex said, "I'm fine, Mr. Smith. I was wondering, do you still have those mice in your cellar?"

"As a matter of fact yes, why do you ask?"

Rex answered, "Well I'm sure that Midnight here wouldn't mind taking care of that problem."

Mr. Smith asked "Would you mind Midnight?" to which he said, "No of course not , I mean after all I am cat and cats are experts at chasing mice and rats away."

Next they went to Mr. Laden's place, and when Mr. Laden saw them he said "What's going on?" to which the dog said, "Mr. Laden, do you still have that rat problem here in your garden?"

Mr. Laden did indeed saying "Sorry to say I do. I've tried everything and nothing works." Then Rex said, "Well I'm sure that Bright Eyes here won't mind helping you keep those pests away." And just like Mr. Smith, Mr. Laden said "Do you mind, Bright Eyes?" And of course, Bright Eyes told him he didn't mind at all.

Lastly they went to Mr. Mitchell's farm, and when they got there Mr. Mitchell was in his barn putting on the finishing touches for the party which was back on. He saw the dog and Bandit and said, "Oh it's you, you know you're way early, the party is not until this evening."

Rex was so surprised "Really? A party for me? Well, I am very surprised. And by the way, do you still have that mouse problem around?"

Mr. Mitchell admitted "Sadly I do." So Rex said "Well I think Bandit here can take care of that for you." Bandit said "It would be my pleasure, Mr. Mitchell."

So Rex left Bandit, Midnight, and Bight Eyes at the three houses. On his way back, he stopped by Mr. Smith's house to see how Midnight was doing. When he got there Midnight was just coming out of the house. The dog went over to him and said "Wow, you were right, I chased away every single mouse that was in his cellar. He was so happy, in fact, he gave me a saucer of milk as a reward."

The dog said, "Really?"

Then Midnight answered, "Really. He said I earned it for getting rid of those mice."

Rex said "See, I told you. Just use what you have and put it to good use."

When he finally got back to his house, he went to go and tell all the boys and girls that the party was back on, and that they should all get ready for this evening. So for the rest of the day, as Mr. Laden and Mr. Smith returned the gallows to the next town over, everybody in town got dressed in their best clothes for the party that evening.

It was just then that the dog realized he had left his hat, bandana, and boots at the sheriff's office. He had forgotten to take them after the fake hanging. Just as he was starting to get nervous, Al came over with the boots, hat, and bandana. When he saw all of the stuff he said, "Thanks Al, I totally forgot I left the stuff at your office. I'm really sorry."

Of course Al sad "There's no need to be sorry. It was an honest mistake."

Later on, after everybody was ready, the dog wondered how he was going to get all of them to the party without losing anybody. But then he had a great idea: he went back to the house and called up Mr. Smith. He asked if he could come to his house in his flat bed truck so that he can all the girls and boys to the party with him leading the way on his zebra.

No more than ten minutes had passed, when Mr. Smith showed up in his flatbed truck. The boys and girls all got on and they head out to the party. When they got to

Mr. Mitchell's farm, Rex was surprised to see the barn all

dark and creepy looking, but he knew it was part of the

party being a surprise. So he went in with all of the boys

and girls right by his side.

At that very moment, the lights went on and

everybody yelled "Surprise." The dog was so touched—

and even surprised— he could hardly speak. Not only was

everybody in town there, but even Bandit, Midnight, and

Bright Eyes showed up. After Rex got over the shock he

said "So what's the occasion for this party?"

Mr. Mitchell said, " For you, Rex. You help

everybody so much, we wanted to show our appreciation.

We thought a party was the best way to do it." The party

was in full swing with everyone eating, drinking, and

dancing. Everyone was singing songs like "Bingo", "How

Much Is That Doggie In The Window", and "Who Let The Dogs Out."

Bandit came over to Rex said "Guess what? Mr. Mitchell appreciated so much how I helped him with the mice in his barn, that he has decided that he wants me around all the time."

The dog said "That's great Bandit, that means he wants you as a pet.

Bandit couldn't believe it, "Really you think so?" to which Rex answered "I know so."

Later on Bright Eyes came by and said, "Listen I know that Midnight, Bandit, and myself haven't been very nice and I just wanted to say that we're really sorry."

Rex thanked him for saying so and asked "And how did things go with Mr. Laden?"

Bright Eyes said, "Better than I thought. Mr. Laden said the time that Jackson and you were playing ball made him realize that he really wanted a pet too. And even though most cats don't like to exercise, he thinks he would have like to me as a pet."

Rex said, "That's great. And Bandit is going to be Mr. Mitchell's pet. He just said he wants him around all of the time to keep the mice out of his barn."

The party ended, and Mr. Smith helped the boys and girls back to the house. And everything was finally back to normal. The cats learned how being nice brings good rewards. And even the bullies learned how to be nice to each other. And all thanks to a yellow dog named Rex.

The End

About The Author

Author Carin Fox was born and raised in the Bronx, New York. She has been writing short stories and poetry since high school, often using animals in domestic situations as a metaphor for humans and their own difficulties.

Her first longer work was **UNUSUAL FAMILY**, about a rock band of 4 seals— all brothers— who are trying to make a record deal. Carin continued the adventures of the 4 musical brothers in her second book **4 SEALS BROTHERS** which begins when the band is signed by a big record producer, who happens to be an octopus. **WESTERN DOG** is Carin's newest work.

Carin is also very active in supporting the Muscular Dystrophy Association, a condition she has fought valiantly and successfully since birth. Part of the proceeds from this book will go to MDA.

She lives happily in the Bronx with her sister Robin and their father Bernard... and she dedicates this work to her late mother Beverly.

Made in the USA
San Bernardino, CA
21 January 2019